THE BOOK THAT BLEEDS

THE LEGEND OF ORIN VESPER

BALI TANU

Copyright © 2025 Bali Tanuj

First Edition: 2025

Cover design by Bali Tanuj

Published by [Independently published]

For permissions, contact: [tanujb214@gmail. com]

TABLE OF CONTENTS

DEDICATION

To the ones who see shadows in mirrors— and still choose to look deeper.

To those who were forgotten, but never stopped remembering themselves.

This is for you.

And for the darkness you survived.

TRIGGER WARNING

This book contains scenes that may be disturbing to some readers, including themes of psychological trauma, identity crisis, existential dread, violence, and emotional distress.

It explores dark imagery, unsettling realities, and elements of horror and gothic suspense.

Reader discretion is advised.

PROLOGUE: THE WHISPER IN THE GLASS

Orin Vesper woke up in a room he didn't remember falling asleep in. It was quiet — too quiet. Not the peaceful kind… the wrong kind.

The air felt heavy, like the silence had weight. Light from the window was thin and pale, barely reaching the floor.

Across the room stood a tall mirror. Cracked. Old. And bleeding.

A line of red ran slowly down its glass — not paint, not dust. It looked exactly like blood.

Orin stared at his reflection. Something was off. The version of him in the mirror smiled… but he wasn't smiling.

Then the reflection blinked. Once. And whispered,

"You don't remember. But you will. "

Orin froze. The voice didn't sound human. It sounded old. Cold. Like it had been waiting.

A chill ran through him. The silence shattered. Not with a sound — but with a feeling.

Something had changed.

CHAPTER 1: THE TOWN WITHOUT A PAST

When Orin stepped outside, the sky was gray but still. The streets of Duskwick were narrow and oddly clean. Too clean.

Nobody smiled. Nobody waved. And yet… everyone seemed to know him.

He walked past the bakery. The smell of bread was there but the windows were blacked out. Past the post office. No letters ever came.

At the corner of the street, an old man sweeping the ground looked up sharply.

"You touched it, didn't you?" the man asked, staring at Orin's hand. "What?"

"The mirror. You touched it. "

The man's broom fell. His eyes widened. "Get out before it remembers you. "

Before Orin could reply, the man turned and slammed his door shut.

Orin kept walking, unsettled. Everything about Duskwick felt off. It was like a dream that had forgotten it was a dream.

Then, around the next corner, it appeared. The Thirteenth House.

Twisted. Old. Dark. A place no one ever talked about. Yet somehow, every road led back to it. No matter which street he took.

Its windows were black mirrors. And inside them — Orin saw himself… even though he was outside.

Something was wrong with this town. Very wrong.

CHAPTER 2: THE MESSAGE IN THE MIRROR

Back at home, Orin stood in front of the mirror again. The blood was still there, sliding slowly across the cracked glass.

He reached out. Touched it. Warm.

Sticky. Real.

Then suddenly — a flash.

A girl laughing. A faceless man. A book burning in fire.

Orin gasped. The images vanished as fast as they came. His head throbbed. His heart raced.

Then, behind the mirror, something scratched into the frame appeared: "To awaken the story, you must bleed into it. "

A knock sounded at the door. He turned — no one there.

But on the floor was a single page. Torn. Faded. It had five words: "Chapter One — The Mirror That Bled. "

CHAPTER 3: THE HOUSE THAT WATCHES

The next day, the Thirteenth House was closer. Across the street from his own door. Like it had moved during the night.

Orin walked toward it.

The path was black stone. The door creaked open by itself. Inside, it was dark, but not empty.

He stepped in.

The house felt bigger than it looked. Walls twisted in strange angles.

Paintings blinked. A clock ticked backward.

Then he found the room. A circular library, silent and full of dust. On a pedestal sat a book with no title. He opened it.

Page one:

“This is the story of Orin Vesper, the boy who broke the mirror. ”

Page two:

“But he is not the first. Nor the last. ” Page three:

Blank. Until blood rose up from the page itself. And wrote: "Chapter Four — The Tale of the Red Queen. "

Orin stepped back. The room darkened. Behind him, the door had vanished.

CHAPTER 4: THE TALE OF THE RED QUEEN

The words on the page bled slowly.

Chapter Four — The Tale of the Red Queen.

Before Orin could blink, the room began to shift. The shelves of books bent sideways. The walls stretched like they were breathing.

Then — a snap.

Like a thread breaking. And the floor disappeared.

He hit the ground hard. But it wasn't the library anymore. It was a forest.

Trees rose high around him, but none had leaves — only red ribbons, tied like veins along the branches. The air was warm, but smelled like rust and roses.

In the distance: laughter. Childlike. Wrong.

He stood and followed the sound.

The path was made of doll parts — porcelain arms and broken legs crushed into dust beneath his steps. Crows watched from the trees, silent and still.

Then he saw her.

At the center of a clearing stood a throne of thorns. And on it sat a girl in a red dress, skin pale as wax, lips cut into a permanent smile.

Her eyes were glass.

Orin knew without knowing — this was her. The Red Queen.

She didn't move at first. Then her voice came, not from her mouth… but from all around him.

“Welcome to my chapter, Orin Vesper. You opened the book. Now you must finish the story. ”

Orin stepped back. “What are you?

She stood.

Behind her, a mirror floated in the air, bleeding like the one at home — only faster, thicker. And in its reflection, Orin didn’t see himself.

He saw a boy with a red hood… and a wolf’s jaw in his hands. The Queen tilted her head.

“You came here for answers. But stories demand sacrifice. ” The trees groaned. The ground cracked. A low growl echoed.

“Let me show you what I once was…”

The mirror began to shimmer, and Orin was pulled toward it — not with force, but with a memory he couldn’t stop.

He reached out.

And everything went black.

CHAPTER 5: ONCE, THERE WAS A GIRL

Once upon a time, in a kingdom that no longer exists, there was a girl born during a blood moon.

She had no name.

Her mother died in silence. Her father never spoke again.

And the midwife who delivered her was found drowned in red water three nights later.

They called the baby cursed.

They said her soul was stitched from broken oaths.

But the King kept her — locked away in the highest tower. Not for her safety.

But for theirs.

She never saw the sky.

Instead, she stared into a mirror. A gift from the Queen. A mirror that whispered stories in her sleep.

Stories of what she should be. A queen. A goddess. A monster.

She believed every word.

On her thirteenth birthday, the court threw a ball. Not for her — for her brother, the golden prince. She was not invited.

But she came anyway, dressed in red, her lips sewn shut with black thread to keep her quiet.

When she entered, the music stopped. The Queen screamed.

The guests fled.

The guards raised their swords. But none struck.

Because behind the girl in red — the mirror followed.

And from its glass stepped out her reflection — twisted, sharp, full of teeth.

That night, the palace burned.

Only one thing remained untouched:

The throne — now made of rose thorns — and the girl in red, smiling wide as she crowned herself.

"You locked me in a tower," she whispered, unsewing her lips. "Now I'll lock your stories in me. "

And so she did.

The kingdom vanished from maps. No one remembered her name.

But fairy tales began to change. They ended differently.

Darker.

Like someone else had taken the pen.

Back in the clearing, Orin gasped.

The mirror shattered beside him. The Red Queen stood silently.

But this time, she wasn't looking at him.

She was looking past him. At something coming.

"You woke me, Orin Vesper," she said softly. "But I am only the first. "

CHAPTER 6: THE BOOK WAKES TOO

Orin woke up on the library floor.

The house was silent, but the silence felt. . . heavier. Like the walls were listening now.

His hands shook as he pushed himself up. The mirror — the one that had floated above the Red Queen's throne was gone.

But the book still sat on the pedestal.

Only now… it was open to a new page. The ink was still wet.

Chapter Five — Complete.

Underneath it, in fresh blood:

Chapter Six: The Man in the Paper Mask

Orin stepped back. The name rang in his head like a bell he'd never heard before — and yet somehow remembered.

His pulse raced.

He turned to leave, but the library door was gone again. Not closed. Not hidden. Erased.

In its place, a new mirror hung on the wall. Smaller. Oval. Cracked at the center like a spiderweb.

Orin's reflection stared back. Then blinked.

But this time… it wasn't him.

The man in the mirror wore a paper-white mask. No mouth. No eyes.

Just blank.

And behind that mask — something moved. Orin froze.

Scratch. A sound came from inside the walls. Then another.

Then… laughter. Dry. Childlike. Far too close. The book flipped a page on its own.

A single sentence had written itself:

"If you want to live, don't turn around. " He didn't.

But something behind him breathed.

After what felt like hours, the sound faded. Orin opened his eyes. The mirror had gone dark again.

The door was back.

He grabbed the book and ran.

Out of the Thirteenth House. Out of the whispering halls. Back into the streets of Duskwick.

Only this time… people were watching.

Every window had eyes now.

Every face looked older than it should.

And in the town square, a page fluttered on the ground the same parchment as the book.

Orin picked it up.

It had no words.

Only a drawing.

A man in a blank paper mask. Standing behind… him.

CHAPTER 7: THE MAN IN THE PAPER MASK

It started with a name. Orin didn't know how he knew it — no one ever told him — but as he stared at the drawing, a whisper brushed his mind:

"Lorian. "

Not spoken aloud.

Not imagined.

Just. . . known.

Lorian. The Man in the Paper Mask.

It rained in Duskwick that night. But not water. Ash.

Fine, pale flakes drifted from a sky with no clouds. The townspeople walked beneath it as if nothing were wrong their skin grey, eyes distant. As if they were all forgetting something together.

Orin moved through the streets with the book tucked in his coat.

Wherever he went, he felt watched. But not from around him. From beneath.

The drains hissed. The grates trembled.

And in every puddle, his reflection wore a mask.

That night, in his room, Orin set the book down and opened it to the next chapter.

Chapter Seven: The Man in the Paper Mask

"He who erased his own soul, so no one could use it against him. " As his fingers touched the page, the candles blew out.

A Memory — Not His Own: It is years ago.

Another city. Another time.

You see Lorian, a boy who never spoke. Because when he did, people forgot things. Dangerous things.

Their names. Their homes. Their children.

So he sewed his lips shut with golden wire, and wore a mask of parchment covered in runes — drawn in his own blood — to keep his identity safe.

Not for protection. But for power.

He could steal memories now.

With a glance.

With a whisper.

With silence.

And the more he took… the less of himself remained.

Until one day, he vanished completely. Not died. Not escaped.

Erased.

Only the mask was left — drifting in a forgotten alley, waiting for another soul to pick it up.

Back in the present:

Orin looked in the mirror again.

For a split second… his mouth was sewn shut. He blinked. Gone. The book flipped itself again. A question had appeared:

"Do you want to know how this story ends?"

Underneath it, a second line began writing in black ink — slowly, deliberately.

Then find the next Chapter. ”

“Before it finds you. ”

CHAPTER 8: THE HOUSE THAT BREATHES

It started with a cough.

Not Orin's.

The walls.

The hallway outside his room began to pulse faintly — not like wind or plumbing...but like lungs.

Inhale.

Exhale.

The wallpaper rippled.

The floorboards creaked, not from footsteps — but from bones shifting underneath.

Orin grabbed the book. It was already open.

Chapter Eight — The House That Breathes

"It doesn't want you to leave. Because you already did."

He tried to run.

But the hallway wasn't the hallway anymore.

It twisted into a long corridor of doors — none he recognized. Each one breathing softly. Some in. Some out.

A child's voice echoed from the end of the hall:

"You left me here."

He froze.

It wasn't just a voice. It was a memory.

His memory.

Flash — A Forgotten Night:

He was ten. Lost in an orphanage that didn't exist on any map.

The other kids whispered about Room 13 — the door that sometimes appeared, sometimes didn't. They dared each other to knock.

He did.

The door opened into darkness. A crib. A crying sound. And then. . . nothing.

He forgot everything that followed. Until now.

The hallway pulsed again.

One of the doors creaked open — not with a squeak, but a gasp. Inside: a nursery.

Rotting wallpaper. Mobiles made of teeth.

And in the crib…something small. Something breathing.

Orin stepped closer.

The thing in the crib wasn't a child. Not anymore.

Its limbs were wood. Its eyes were sewn shut. But its chest rose and fell like lungs filled with smoke.

It sat up.

"You left me here, brother. "

Orin stumbled back. "No… I don't—" The floor split open like a mouth.

He fell.

Beneath the House:

Orin landed on pages. Thousands of torn pages — children's stories rewritten with violence, blood, and silence.

A woman sat in the center of the pile, rocking something in her arms. A doll. A real one. Its jaw twisted sideways.

The woman's face was blurred, smeared like wet ink. She looked up.

"The House remembers, Orin.

All lost children come home eventually. "

The mirror rose behind her.

A heartbeat pulsed in the glass.

And Orin's reflection was now a boy. Ten years old. Terrified. Holding a doll.

He whispered, "Who are you?" She smiled.

"They called me Mother.

But they sealed me as The House That Breathes.

Because I raised monsters. . . and fed them fairy tales. "

The book snapped shut.

When Orin opened his eyes again, he was back in his room. Sweating.

Shaking.

Alone? No.

Because outside his window, something was watching.

CHAPTER 9: THE PUPPETEER'S SPINE

Orin stopped sleeping.

Every time he closed his eyes, he heard strings tightening. Pulling.

Not from above… But from inside.

His joints ached. His spine itched.

Like something was learning how to wear him.

The book flipped on its own.

Chapter Nine — The Puppeteer's Spine

She doesn't control people. She lets their lies control them. "

The page smelled like copper. And this time, the ink wasn't red.

It was gray.

Like ash and bone.

Somewhere else — not a memory, not a dream:

A theater. Empty.

Marionettes hang from wires above — but they don't dangle. They twitch.

Sway. Breathe.

And in the center aisle walks a girl in a long coat stitched from voices.

Her face is blank, like a porcelain mask cracked down the middle.

She doesn't pull the strings. She whispers to them.

And they move.

Not like puppets. Like people.

Dead people.

Back in Duskwick, Orin finds a single puppet nailed to his door. Its arms bend wrong. Its mouth sewn into a smile.

Pinned to its chest: a note.

“Do you remember what you promised her?” He doesn’t.

But his fingers are already shaking as he turns the page.

Inside the book — the puppeteer’s tale unfolds: They called her Marla, once.

The girl with joints too loose and a spine too straight.

She never lied. Couldn’t. So the world lied to her.

One night, she broke.

One by one, she stitched the liars into puppets. Not as punishment.

As mercy.

Because if they couldn’t lie anymore… They wouldn’t hurt her again.

Now, she wears a crown of fingers.

And listens for anyone who speaks a false word. When they do?

She finds them.

And their truth becomes hers to use.

Present:

Orin opens his mouth to scream. But no sound comes.

Because he's not holding the book anymore.

He's holding strings.

And they're connected to people he knows. People in town. All walking like sleepwalkers.

Because he turned the page.

And now…he's part of the show.

The Hidden Pattern: The Circle of Unmaking

The Forgotten Thirteen weren't sealed randomly.

They represent a cosmic order in reverse — a ritual of uncreation, masked as fairy tales, stitched through horror.

This is known as the:

Circle of Unmaking

A forbidden myth that unwinds the world one forgotten truth at a time. Each of the Thirteen embodies a reversal of something divine or sacred: Number Forgotten One Reversal Of. . .

1 The Red Queen Creation (rewrites origin)

2 The Man in the Paper Mask Memory (erases identity)

3 The House That Breathes Family (twists motherhood)

4 The Puppeteer's Spine Free Will (manipulates truth)

5 The Clock That Ticks Backwards Time (reverses fate)

6 The Bride in Black Lace Love (devours devotion)

7 The Conductor of Screams Sound (turns music into madness)

8 The Child Who Never Died Death (defies endings)

9 The Queen of Salt Nature (poisons earth/sea)

10 The Wolf of Many Voices Speech (destroys language)

11 The Storyteller Without a Mouth Meaning (corrupts stories)

12 The Ghost with the Sacred Name Name (erases all reality)

13 Chapter Thirteen (Unknown) God (replaces everything)

The Final Twist:

The order Orin encounters them does not match their number. That's the trap.

Each Forgotten One reveals a glyph, a mark that seems random — until Orin realizes:

The Thirteen are not a list. They are a lock.

And the book… is the key.

If opened in the correct order, it seals them forever. If opened in the wrong order — like now —they awaken. "

CHAPTER 10: THE CLOCK THAT TICKS BACKWARDS

"Time is not a line. It is a room with one locked door — and someone on the other side is turning the handle. "

The clocks in Duskwick all stopped at once. 3:33 AM.

All of them.

Orin saw it first on his wristwatch. Then on his wall.

Then on the street, where every clock tower, vending machine, and shop display froze — hands pointed straight up like they were waiting to fall. But they never moved forward.

Instead…they began to tick backward.

That night, the Book That Bleeds refused to open. Instead, it whispered:

>"You've already read this chapter. You just don't remember yet. "

And on Orin's wall, something new had appeared:

A mirror — thin, oval, and made of rusted metal. Its surface was not glass.

It was mercury — swirling, warping. And within it, he saw himself……aged.

Older. Paler. Eyes hollow.

Holding a clock with no numbers, only scars. The reflection spoke first.

"You need to go back, Orin. Before you finish the Thirteen. "Why?"

"Because one of them… is you. "

A Tear in Time

Suddenly, Orin wasn't in his room anymore.

He stood in a field of dying grass under a moonless sky.

In the center stood a grand clocktower, broken and bleeding sand.

A man sat at its base, building a clock from bones. His face was rotted, but his eyes were kind.

"Welcome, Orin. I've been expecting you. "

"Who are you?"

"The one who failed before you.

The first who tried to open the book in the correct order. "

"You're a Forgotten?"

"No. Worse. "

"I'm what happens when time tries to fix itself. "

The man handed Orin a gear carved with symbols. A single name etched into the brass:Vael.

(The First Clockmaker. The one who unwrote time.)

"He's next," the old man whispered. "But don't make the mistake I did.

When you meet him… don't ask what hour it is. "

Back in the Present… or Maybe the Past: Orin jolted awake.

A new chapter had appeared in the book.

Chapter Ten — The Clock That Ticks Backwards "He didn't die at the end of time. He started it. "

And written underneath, not in ink, but in blood:

"You are out of order. "

Now, Orin knows:

He's reading the book in the wrong sequence. Every step forward awakens, not seals.

And someone — or something — is making sure he never learns the right way.

Until it's too late.

CHAPTER 11: THE BRIDE IN BLACK LACE

She waited at the altar until the world ended.

Then she married the silence. "

Rain swept through Duskwick like needles. Orin hadn't spoken in hours.

Not since the mirror whispered the name: Virelle.

A name that didn't belong in any record, fairy tale, or history. And yet, he knew it.

Like a forgotten melody that still made him weep.

The book bled before it opened.

A lace ribbon fell out — black, wet, and cold as grave dirt.

Chapter Eleven — The Bride in Black Lace

To love her is to vanish. To leave her… is to rot. "

Orin didn't choose to read it. The book chose him.

Flashback – A Wedding That Never Was A grand cathedral under a pale sky.

Dozens of guests. No faces.

Only masks. Weeping. Laughing. Screaming. All sewn shut.

At the altar stood Virelle — the most beautiful horror ever made.

Her dress was stitched from black lace, spider silk, and mourning veils.

She waited.

Waited for her groom to arrive. He never did.

He had run.

And so she stood… for seven centuries.

The bells never rang. The guests never left.

Time turned to mildew, and vows became curses.

She no longer remembers his face. Only his absence.

Now, she marries anyone who wanders near. And if they leave her…

They vanish.

Not die. Not rot.

They are unwritten — their memories scraped from every page, every person, every world.

As if they never were.

Present Day — Orin's Dilemma

Orin finds a chapel in Duskwick that wasn't there yesterday. At its doors, a note:

"You came back. "

He enters.

Candles flicker. No wind.

A mirror waits at the altar — tall, obsidian, veiled in black lace. And beside it, a bridal mannequin.

It turns to face him.

Her voice is the sound of silk ripping in a grave

Will you leave me too, Orin?"

He wants to run.

But his feet are already rooted. The book writes itself:

One does not escape the Bride. One weds her — or forgets they ever were. "

The Choice

Orin has to pretend to love her until the book finishes the chapter. One wrong word… and his entire existence is erased. He walks forward.

Takes her lace-covered hand.

And says the most terrifying thing he's ever said:

I missed you. "She smiles. And weeps ink. The lace lifts from the mirror, revealing Orin's reflection…standing alone at the altar. No bride.

No chapel. No world.

He's back in his room.

But now, something is missing. A photo frame.

His mother's name in his phone.

The sound of laughter in his memory. He loved someone once. But they're gone.

The book closes.

A whisper from its spine:

"Three more seals, Orin.

Then the mirror will show your true name. "

CHAPTER 12: THE STORYTELLER WITHOUT A MOUTH

"He wrote the end of every tale.

Until someone tore out his tongue. "

Duskwick is almost unrecognizable now. The sky bleeds rust instead of clouds.

Children draw with chalk, but the drawings whisper when walked upon.

No one speaks names anymore — only gestures, as if the sound of identity has become dangerous.

And every storybook in every house has the same final sentence:

"He watched them forget, and wept without a sound. "

The book won't open.

Instead, Orin finds a single page nailed to his window.

It's not written.

It's etched in scars:

Chapter Twelve — The Storyteller Without a Mouth
"He gave the world meaning. And was silenced for it. "

The Tale Unfolds

Long ago, before the Thirteen were sealed, one being held them together — not by power, but by narrative.

A storyteller. He didn't speak to rule. He spoke to remember. But when the Forgotten began to turn on one another, they realized something horrifying:

If no one tells the tale… the tale ends.

So they cut out his tongue.

They stitched his mouth shut with thread made from cursed names. They burned every pen he ever touched.

But stories… do not die. They rot.

And return.

Now, he writes with blood on walls. He draws in riddles and wounds.

He lives in the space between words — where meaning goes to scream. And he has written something… for Orin.

The Encounter

At the edge of Duskwick, Orin finds a library that should not exist. Every book is blank.

Except one.

A thin black journal on a pedestal, vibrating softly. When Orin opens it, words bloom across the page:

>“You are almost the last sentence.

But you’ve been speaking someone else’s story. ”

Suddenly, all pages turn. The final one reads:

“The Storyteller gave his tongue to seal the Thirteen. You must give something greater to end them. ”

A reflection appears — but this time, Orin doesn’t see himself. He sees a child.

With no face.

Holding a quill made of bone. Writing in a voice that doesn't exist.

And on the next page appears a phrase:

“To finish the book… you must become the one who

forgets. "Orin looks up.

The world is screaming without sound.

People's mouths are moving, but there are no voices. He can't hear his own heartbeat.

The chapter ends in silence.

What Orin Has Lost

In Chapter 4 — The House That Breathes — we saw a crib. We never looked inside.

In Chapter 6 — The Man in the Paper Mask — we read a memory erased.

We never asked whose.

In Chapter 11 — The Bride in Black Lace — someone vanished from Orin's world.

We assumed it was a lover.

But all along… it was his brother.

The Forgotten Twin Orin Vesper had a twin.

Born minutes apart under a cursed blood moon.

Two infants — one screamed, one stared silently. The town midwife warned:

One will bring words. The other… silence. "

So they hid the second child. No name. No birtcertificate. No stories.

And when the sealing began, that child was taken — as the thirteenth sacrifice to seal the final Forgotten.

They didn't kill him. They wrote him out.

The Book's True Purpose

The Book That Bleeds is not a diary. It's not a cursed

fairy tale. It is the coffin of Orin's brother.

Each chapter Orin reads doesn't just awaken a Forgotten it unseals a fragment of his twin's erased existence.

But the cost? Every time he learns more, he forgets something else. His mother's face. His birthday. The first lie he ever told.

Because to remember his brother, Orin must become less of himself. Until there's nothing left… but the one who rewrites God.

The Final Truth Before Chapter 13 Orin isn't the hero of the story. He's the lock. His brother… is the key.

And the book has tricked them both.

CHAPTER 13: THE ONE THAT REWRITES GOD

The first story ever told was not a creation.

It was an erasure. "The Book That Bleeds no longer rests on Orin's desk. It floats.

Pages turning by themselves, ink dripping upward, symbols rearranging faster than thought.

Outside, the sky is cracked glass. People walk on ceilings.

Clocks strike names instead of hours. And in the center of Duskwick…a boy stands barefoot in the rain.

He looks like Orin. Younger.

Eyes darker than time. No shadow.

And when Orin finally speaks:"You're my brother. "

The boy does not smile. He hands Orin the final page. It is blank. The Ritual of Reversal

Each Forgotten was sealed by a truth twisted into myth. Now, with all seals undone, the truth returns — and it burns.

The boy says only one word:"Write.

But Orin's hands won't move. His voice is gone.

Because now, he remembers:

He was never supposed to exist. The original sacrifice was him — but his brother took his place. The book was meant to rewrite Orin out of the world. But it failed.

The Final Choice A new pen appears. Made of bone.

Ink made of Orin's memories. He has two choices:

1 Write his brother back into the world, fully — making him real, undoing the curse — but in doing so, Orin will vanish.

2 Rewrite the book to seal the Forgotten again, preserving himself — but condemning his twin to eternal non-existence.

The page waits. The book pulses. The world flickers. And Orin… Begins to write.

Finale — The Author Who Never Was

Orin Vesper dipped the bone-pen into the ink of his own memory.

Names bled from his skin — his first word, the scent of his father, the laughter he once carried.

He wrote…

"Let there be one who was forgotten. Let there be one who was loved. "And the moment the final word was written, he was gone.

Across Duskwick…The sky stitched itself shut. Time snapped back like a broken spine. Mirrors stopped whispering.

Clocks began to tick forward again. The chapel vanished.

The silent library turned to ash. The Book That Bleeds… crumbled to dust.

A boy now stands at the edge of the town. No one remembers his name.

But they smile when they see him. Because deep down, their hearts know:

"Someone gave everything… so I could be real. "

He walks past places he has never seen, yet somehow knows — beneath the skin of the world, in the marrow of fate — he was loved by a ghost.

In a Forgotten Corner of the World. . . A single page remains.

Burned. Torn. Faded. But it still holds words.

Scrawled in a child's hand:

"This story was written in silence. And ended in love. "

Beneath it, a name no one remembers: Orin Vesper.

Epilogue — The Book That Breathes

Years later, in a home with no clocks, a child finds something buried under the floorboards.

A blank book. On the last page, in a voice that does not exist:"Do not write your name.

Unless you are ready to be forgotten. "

And thus ends the legend of Orin Vesper, The Author Who Never Was,

The One Who Gave Up His Story… To Give Another One Life. For Readers

www.ingramcontent.com/pod-product-compliance
Lightning Source LLC
Chambersburg PA
CBHW050026170726
48282CB00025B/572

* 9 7 8 9 3 3 4 3 2 4 7 0 9 *